The Little
Red Hen

First published in 2006 by
Franklin Watts
338 Euston Road
London
NW1 3BH

Franklin Watts Australia
Hachette Children's Books
Level 17/207 Kent Street
Sydney
NSW 2000

Text © Penny Dolan 2006
Illustration © Beccy Blake 2006

A CIP catalogue record for this book is available
from the British Library.

ISBN 0 7496 6578 5 (hbk)
ISBN 0 7496 6585 8 (pbk)

Series Editor: Jackie Hamley
Series Advisor: Dr Barrie Wade
Series Designer: Peter Scoulding

Printed in China

The Little Red Hen

Retold by Penny Dolan

Illustrated by Beccy Blake

FRANKLIN WATTS
LONDON•SYDNEY

Little Red Hen found some grains of wheat.

"Who will help me plant them?" asked Little Red Hen.

"Not I!"
said Cat.

"Not I!"
said Dog.

"Not I!"
said Rat.

9

The wheat grew, but
the weeds grew, too.
"Who will help me weed?"
asked Little Red Hen.

"Not I!" said Cat.
"Not I!" said Dog.
"Not I!" said Rat.

11

"Then I must do it myself!"
she said.

The wheat grew ripe.

"Who will help me cut the wheat?" asked Little Red Hen.

"Not I!" yawned Cat.

"Not I!" yawned Dog.

"Not I!" yawned Rat.

"Then I must harvest it myself," she said.

"Who will help me carry the wheat?" asked Little Red Hen.

"Not I!" grumbled Cat.

"Not I!" grumbled Dog.

"Not I!" grumbled Rat.

"Then I must carry it to the mill myself," she said.

The miller ground the
wheat into flour.

"Who will help me make and bake my bread?" asked Little Red Hen.

yeast

FLOUR

22

Nobody answered.
"Then I will make
and bake it myself!"

Cat, Dog and Rat smelt
something delicious.

25

"Who will help me eat my bread?" called Little Red Hen.

"Me!" said Cat.
"Me!" said Dog.
"Me, me, me!" said Rat.

"Who is asking you?"
laughed Little Red Hen.

29

"I am calling all my little chicks to help me eat my bread!"

Leapfrog has been specially designed to fit the requirements of the National Literacy Strategy. It offers real books for beginning readers by top authors and illustrators.

There are 49 Leapfrog stories to choose from:

The Bossy Cockerel
ISBN 0 7496 3828 1

Bill's Baggy Trousers
ISBN 0 7496 3829 X

Mr Spotty's Potty
ISBN 0 7496 3831 1

Little Joe's Big Race
ISBN 0 7496 3832 X

The Little Star
ISBN 0 7496 3833 8

The Cheeky Monkey
ISBN 0 7496 3830 3

Selfish Sophie
ISBN 0 7496 4385 4

Recycled!
ISBN 0 7496 4388 9

Felix on the Move
ISBN 0 7496 4387 0

Pippa and Poppa
ISBN 0 7496 4386 2

Jack's Party
ISBN 0 7496 4389 7

The Best Snowman
ISBN 0 7496 4390 0

Eight Enormous Elephants
ISBN 0 7496 4634 9

Mary and the Fairy
ISBN 0 7496 4633 0

The Crying Princess
ISBN 0 7496 4632 2

Jasper and Jess
ISBN 0 7496 4081 2

The Lazy Scarecrow
ISBN 0 7496 4082 0

The Naughty Puppy
ISBN 0 7496 4383 8

Freddie's Fears
ISBN 0 7496 4382 X

FAIRY TALES

Cinderella
ISBN 0 7496 4228 9

The Three Little Pigs
ISBN 0 7496 4227 0

Jack and the Beanstalk
ISBN 0 7496 4229 7

The Three Billy Goats Gruff
ISBN 0 7496 4226 2

Goldilocks and the Three Bears
ISBN 0 7496 4225 4

Little Red Riding Hood
ISBN 0 7496 4224 6

Rapunzel
ISBN 0 7496 6159 3

Snow White
ISBN 0 7496 6161 5

The Emperor's New Clothes
ISBN 0 7496 6163 1

The Pied Piper of Hamelin
ISBN 0 7496 6164 X

Hansel and Gretel
ISBN 0 7496 6162 3

The Sleeping Beauty
ISBN 0 7496 6160 7

Rumpelstiltskin
ISBN 0 7496 6165 8

The Ugly Duckling
ISBN 0 7496 6166 6

Puss in Boots
ISBN 0 7496 6167 4

The Frog Prince
ISBN 0 7496 6168 2

The Princess and the Pea
ISBN 0 7496 6169 0

Dick Whittington
ISBN 0 7496 6170 4

The Elves and the Shoemaker
ISBN 0 7496 6575 0*
ISBN 0 7496 6581 5

The Little Match Girl
ISBN 0 7496 6576 9*
ISBN 0 7496 6582 3

The Little Mermaid
ISBN 0 7496 6577 7*
ISBN 0 7496 6583 1

The Little Red Hen
ISBN 0 7496 6578 5*
ISBN 0 7496 6585 8

The Nightingale
ISBN 0 7496 6579 3*
ISBN 0 7496 6586 6

Thumbelina
ISBN 0 7496 6580 7*
ISBN 0 7496 6587 4

RHYME TIME

Squeaky Clean
ISBN 0 7496 6588 2*
ISBN 0 7496 6805 9

Craig's Crocodile
ISBN 0 7496 6589 0*
ISBN 0 7496 6806 7

Felicity Floss: Tooth Fairy
ISBN 0 7496 6590 4*
ISBN 0 7496 6807 5

Captain Cool
ISBN 0 7496 6591 2*
ISBN 0 7496 6808 3

Monster Cake
ISBN 0 7496 6592 0*
ISBN 0 7496 6809 1

The Super Trolley Ride
ISBN 0 7496 6593 9*
ISBN 0 7496 6810 5

* hardback